MW00809648

Suzanne Kamata

BAKE SALE

Suzanne Kamata is a teacher of English as a Foreign Language and an award-winning author. Her books include *The Spy*, *A Girls' Guide to the Islands*, *Gadget Girl*, and *Indigo Girl*. Although she is an American and loves France, she lives in Tokushima, Japan.

First published by Gemma in 2022.

GemmaMedia | Gemma Open Door for Literacy
230 Commercial Street
Boston MA 02109

www.gemmamedia.org

Printed in the United States of America

978-1-956476-18-7

Library of Congress Cataloging-in-Publication Data
Names: Kamata, Suzanne, 1965- author.
Title: Bake sale / Suzanne Kamata.
Description: Boston : GemmaMedia, 2022. | Series: Gemma Open Door
Identifiers: LCCN 2022037275 (print) | LCCN 2022037276 (ebook) | ISBN
   9781956476187 (paperback) | ISBN 9781956476194 (ebook)
Classification: LCC PS3611.A465 B35 2022 (print) | LCC PS3611.A465
   (ebook) | DDC 813/.6--dc23
LC record available at https://lccn.loc.gov/2022037275
LC ebook record available at https://lccn.loc.gov/2022037276

Cover by Laura Shaw Design

Gemma's Open Doors provide fresh stories, new ideas, and essential resources for young people and adults as they embrace the power of reading and the written word.

Open Door

– 1 –

Dr. Laura Murata stepped into her Tokyo apartment. Her seven-year-old daughter Maya trailed behind her. In one hand, she held a briefcase. It was filled with fifty university students' essays. Laura needed to grade them ASAP. In the other hand, she clutched a bag of fast food from a popular Korean chain.

Laura was so hungry. She had not had time to eat lunch. But first she needed to change out of her suit. If she got ketchup on it, she wouldn't be able to wear it again until it was dry-cleaned.

Maya marched to her room. She changed out of the blazer and skirt that she wore. It was the uniform for Tokyo Cherry Blossom International School.

She put on a pink sweatshirt, a white tutu, and sparkly leggings.

Laura changed into jeans and a flannel shirt. She arranged the burgers and salads on plates. She felt guilty about serving her girl takeout three days in a row. They would have fresh fruit for dessert.

Maya sat down at the table. Laura took a big bite of her burger.

"Mom," Maya said. "I almost forgot. My teacher said to remind you about tomorrow's holiday bake sale."

Oh no. Laura squeezed her eyes shut. She gently pounded her forehead with her fist.

"Are you okay, Mom?"

Laura forced a smile. "Uh, yes! Thank you so much for the reminder!"

Of course, she had forgotten. Of course, she had ignored yesterday's group message from the PTA president. The message had probably been about the bake sale.

Laura sighed. What kind of cookies should she make?

– 2 –

Last year, Laura sent along Rice Krispie Treats for the bake sale. She loved them when she was a kid in Michigan. Most people did. Laura thought that she had made a good choice.

As she melted marshmallows at the stove, she remembered her childhood. Her mother wore a floral apron while baking. She put cookies into a cookie jar shaped like a giant strawberry. From the kitchen window in Michigan, they could see rabbits and deer.

Laura poured the cereal into the melted marshmallows. She folded in green and red M&M's. She scraped it all into a pan. When it had cooled, she cut it into squares. She covered it with plastic wrap. Finally, she bundled it into a *furoshiki*—a traditional Japanese wrapping cloth. When she dropped Maya off at the school gate, she handed her the bundle. "Here, give this to your teacher for the holiday bake sale."

Laura was sure it would be a big hit. She had never met a kid who didn't like Rice Krispie Treats. The American parents would probably feel nostalgic. The Japanese parents might be interested in the treats because they were made of rice. Everyone in Japan liked rice.

Laura had not been able to help out with the bake sale because of her job. Most of the mothers were stay-at-home moms. Their husbands made a lot of money. Laura was a single mother. She did her best to provide for her daughter.

Maya's dad was Japanese. Since the divorce, he had started another family. He hardly ever saw Maya. He rarely sent money.

Laura went to the women's university where she taught. She walked with a spring in her step. She had done her duty. There would be no guilt trips from teachers and PTA moms this year. She spent the day teaching her students how to write a perfect paragraph. In another class, she and her students had a discussion about current events. They talked about companies that required their female employees to wear high heels. After her classes finished, she went to pick up her daughter from school. She was still in a good mood.

When she arrived at the school, Maya seemed sad. She was holding the bundle. Her homeroom teacher, Ms. Maeda, was next to her. The teacher was frowning.

3

"What happened?" Laura asked.

"I'm sorry, Murata-san," Ms. Maeda said. "We couldn't put your cake out at the bake sale like this. You should have wrapped each piece in plastic. Or maybe paper."

"Oh, it's not cake," Laura began. She stopped when she saw Ms. Maeda's pained expression. She had messed up. She had let down the PTA. And Maya was disappointed.

"For hygiene's sake," Ms. Maeda gently added.

"Oh yes, of course," Laura said. She could feel the blood filling her face. "I should have known better. I won't let it happen again."

Laura had felt very guilty. This year she had volunteered to bake cookies. She would also sell the baked goods.

Now she had less than twelve hours. What should she bake?

Why oh why hadn't she remembered this sooner? She and Maya could have spent Saturday afternoon baking cookies together, just as she and her mother had done.

They did not have enough flour or sugar. They would have to go shopping. Or she could go to the American bakery down the street.

The cookies would probably be expensive. But would the PTA really care that she had cheated? She vowed that she would bake her own cookies next year to make up for it. She would choose the most difficult recipe that she could find. But this time, it could not be helped.

"Maya," Laura said. "Let's make a quick run to Emily's Sweet Shop."

Maya frowned. "You mean you're not going to bake cookies for tomorrow?"

"Not this time, honey," Laura said. "But don't tell, okay?"

4

They pulled on jackets and went out. The evening air was brisk. It was only the end of November, but Christmas decorations were already up.

Christmas was not even a holiday in Japan. Laura had to work on that day. But she loved everything about Christmas. She was happy that it had caught on. The Japanese celebrated Christmas in a different way. Families had fried chicken and Christmas cake. Christmas Eve was a big date night in Japan.

Laura followed Maya. Maya skipped past shops. Christmas lights decorated the windows. Laura could see small Christmas trees with colored bulbs. They passed a clothing boutique and a florist. They came to the bakery. Emily's Sweet Shop was run by an American. A bell tinkled as they entered.

"Hey there," said a woman. She was wearing a kerchief over her short white hair. "Pretty chilly tonight, isn't it?"

Laura nodded. "Got any cookies? There's a bake sale at school tomorrow. I totally forgot!"

Emily laughed. "Do you want something fancy? Or something that looks homemade?"

Laura peered into the case. She saw cakes topped with strawberries. Her mouth watered. Then she spotted a row of candy cane cookies. The cookies looked like the ones she and her mother used to make. She remembered rolling the dough into long strands.

They braided the red and green lengths together.

"Do you have a couple dozen of those?" Laura asked.

Emily nodded. She put on a plastic glove. She began to put the cookies into a box. Laura thought that she had plastic bags at home. She and Maya could put each one in a bag and tie it with a ribbon.

"Well, that's sorted," Laura said. They left the bakery.

"Can I have one when we get home?" Maya asked.

"Okay," Laura said, a sparkle in her eyes. "But just one! You can buy lots of different cookies at the bake sale tomorrow."

– 5 –

The next morning, Laura went with Maya to her classroom.

"I brought cookies," Laura said to the teacher. "Where should I put them?"

This year, Maya's homeroom teacher was a young Canadian. "Thank you so much," said Ms. Cooper. "And you're volunteering today, right?"

"Yes I am," Laura said.

"Did you remember to bring an apron?" Ms. Cooper asked.

"Uh . . ." Laura had forgotten.

"Everyone has to wear one," Ms. Cooper said. "And you should wear a hairnet."

Laura wondered if she had time to go

home and get an apron. Or maybe there was a shop nearby?

Noticing her distress, Ms. Cooper put a hand on her arm. "It's okay if you forgot. One of the other mothers brought an extra."

Sure enough, one of the PTA moms hurried over when she entered the cafeteria. The woman handed Laura an apron and a cotton kerchief.

"You can line up your cookies here," the mom said. She pointed to a space on one of the long tables. The table was covered with a festive tablecloth.

Laura took her time lining up the candy cane cookies.

The kids had made signs. Maya set up the one that she had made. It was decorated with snowflakes. She went to greet her friends after she placed the sign.

A few other women were putting out their own cookies. Laura did not know the other mothers well. She took a look around. A mother from Italy had baked chocolate biscotti. One from India was selling *ladoos*. Another from China advertised moon cakes. Many of the Japanese mothers had baked cut-out cookies. They were dainty and decorated with glitter and jimmies.

She admired some gingerbread boys and girls. Some noise came from the entrance. She looked up to see a Japanese man. Not just a man, but a father. A boy was with him. The man was wearing a University of Oregon sweatshirt. And he was holding a big plastic container.

Was he famous? It was possible. One of the other fathers was a professional golfer who appeared often on TV. Another was a newscaster.

"Dr. Mori, it's so wonderful you could come!" a mother said.

"Wouldn't miss it for the world," he said. He had a perfect American accent. He flashed a smile. "The bake sale is our thing." He ruffled the hair of the boy next to him.

The boy's mother was obviously a foreigner. Laura could always tell.

Suddenly, Maya shot into view. She twirled in front of the boy. Then the two kids took off to another corner of the room. Huh. They must be friends.

– 6 –

Dr. Mori moved toward the tables. He had to lay out his own baked goods.

Laura went back to her table. She waited for the bake sale to begin. Her candy cane cookies were displayed between Mexican wedding cakes and sweet potato tarts.

She greeted the women on either side of her. One looked to be about six months pregnant. She was from Central America. The other was a Japanese woman who was married to an American.

Suddenly, she heard a deep voice. "Hello!"

She looked up into warm brown eyes. "Oh, hello."

"You must be Mrs. Murata," he said.

"Dr. Murata," she said, then blushed. She didn't want him to think that she was arrogant. But she had studied hard to get that PhD.

Dr. Mori seemed confused. He looked at her left ring finger. The finger was bare. Then his eyes went back to her face. "Pardon me. Dr. Murata. Of course."

She checked his finger. Nope, no wedding ring. He might be married, though. A lot of Japanese men didn't wear rings.

"My son talks about your daughter all the time," he said. "I'm Kazu Mori, by the way."

"Oh!" Laura said.

He reached into the front pouch of

his hoodie and pulled out a little case. He opened it. He took out a business card and handed it to Laura.

"Kazu Mori, DDS," she read. He was a dentist. "It's clever of you to go where the sugar is," she said. "These moms will let their kids eat sweet things. Then they will feel guilty and book appointments."

Kazu laughed. "I never thought of it like that. Maybe you're right."

"I'm just kidding." She gave him her own business card. She held out her hand. "It's nice to meet you."

He shook her hand. His grip was firm and warm. She felt heat spread through her fingers. It went up her arm and to her chest. Oh my. Her heart beat faster.

She felt a little disappointed when he let go. Most Japanese people just bowed. There was so little physical contact. She had forgotten how nice it could be.

"These cookies look great, by the way." Kazu said. "Can I buy some now?"

The bake sale would start in twenty minutes, but Laura didn't see the harm. It was fine as long as she sold the cookies and gave the money to the PTA, right?

"Sure," she said.

"Two, please."

She slid two of the individually wrapped cookies into a paper bag. He gave her a few coins. His smile made her knees feel weak.

"Thanks so much," Kazu said. "Come over later and check out my rugelach."

7

Laura watched Kazu walk away. She hoped that she would be able to speak to him again. He had a nice body. But that was not why she wanted to talk to him. She wanted to speak to him for professional reasons.

She was working on a paper on the division of housework in Japan. He would be able to provide valuable data. How many fathers in Japan helped out with school bake sales? At this one, he was the only father. This man was practically a unicorn.

"It's great that Dr. Mori helps his wife," Laura said to the two women beside her.

The Japanese mother gasped. "Didn't you know?" she said. "Dr. Mori is a widower."

"Oh! No, I did not know," Laura said. "Did his wife pass recently?"

"Little Max was a toddler then," the other woman said. She had brought the Mexican wedding cakes. "It has been a while."

"Where was his wife from?" Laura asked. These women seemed to know all about Dr. Mori.

"Poland, I think," the Latina mom said.

"She was ill," the Japanese mother added.

"Poor Dr. Mori," Laura said. The three of them gazed across the room at the man. Another mother handed him a pink ruffled apron. Apparently, he had forgotten his apron, too.

He looked over just then and caught her eye. She smiled. He flashed her a dazzling grin. Once again, she was filled with a warm tingle.

Yes, she definitely needed to check out his rugelach.

Soon the cafeteria was filled with people. The bake sale was open to the public. In addition to the children, parents, and school staff, customers from the community milled about. Laura's cookies sold out quickly. She closed up shop and went to browse the others' baked goods.

When she reached Dr. Mori's table, she saw that he had also sold out.

"No more rugelach?" she asked.

He shrugged. "I'm so sorry. They went like hotcakes. But maybe Max and I can make another batch this weekend."

"You really baked them yourself?" Laura asked.

"Of course," Kazu said. "It was my wife's recipe. Max doesn't remember her well. I try to help him connect with her through stories and food."

He was so sweet. Laura wanted to give him a hug, but she didn't. That would be so odd.

Max showed up just then. "Dad, I want to show you something!" he said. He tugged on his father's hand.

"Talk to you later?" Kazu said. And then he was gone.

8

They had only met briefly, but Laura could not stop thinking about Kazu. That night she read a chapter of *Charlie and the Chocolate Factory* to Maya. Then she tucked her in. She wondered if Kazu was tucking in Max, too. Did he read him a bedtime story? If so, what?

Laura kissed Maya's cheek. She softly closed her bedroom door. She went into the living room. Her phone pinged. There was a text from Kazu. She felt a little flutter in her stomach.

"Those candy cane cookies were amazing!" he wrote. "What is that secret ingredient? Please give me the recipe! Max is begging me for more of these cookies."

Secret ingredient? Oh no. Laura knew of a few recipes for candy cane cookies. But what if they were not the same? She had not had a chance to try one of the cookies herself. She could not imagine what the secret ingredient might be.

True, she had not told anyone that she baked them. Even so, she would be too embarrassed to admit that she bought the cookies She bit her lip for a moment, thinking.

"Better yet, how about if I bring you a freshly baked batch of cookies?" she texted. He would appreciate that, right? As a single father and a dentist, he was a very busy man.

"Great idea," he texted.

Swoon.

"Next Saturday? Why don't you bring Maya over to my place? You and I can have coffee while the kids run around."

Oh, so it was more like a playdate. It was a chance for their kids to hang out together. Still, she was eager to get to know him better. He might be able to supply her with some valuable data for her paper.

"Sounds like a plan," she texted.

He replied with a dancing bear emoji. He sent her a link with directions to his and Max's address.

9

Laura dropped down on the sofa. Dr. Mori had invited her over for coffee! Okay, so it was not a date. It was nothing romantic. Or maybe it could turn out to be?

Then she thought of the cookies. What if he found out that she hadn't actually baked them? Would he think that she was a liar? Maybe she could get Emily to give her the recipe. If she made a batch of cookies herself, she wouldn't feel so bad about her deception.

She dropped by Emily's Sweet Shop the next morning. The bakery smelled like butter, sugar, and spices. Laura saw cookies sprinkled with red and green sugar. But where were the candy cane cookies?

Emily appeared just then. She wiped floury hands on her apron. "Hey Laura. What can I get you today?"

"Did you stop making the candy cane cookies?" Laura asked. She felt slightly panicked.

"No, not at all," Emily said. "I make them every other day."

Phew. "They were amazing," Laura said, quoting Kazu. "Would you be willing to share the recipe?"

Emily chuckled. "You think I am going to give you my secret recipe? You would make them at home and stop buying them from me."

"Well, maybe." Laura smiled sheepishly.

"Not a chance." Emily was sweet, but she was also strong-willed.

"Okay then, could I order a dozen?" Laura asked. "I will pick them up on Friday."

Emily winked. "That's more like it."

10

Laura and Maya put up their Christmas tree on Friday evening. It was a fake tree, but it would have to do. Most of the decorations were homemade.

"Remember this?" Laura asked. She held up a glittery pinecone. It hung from a loop of red yarn.

"Uh, not really," Maya said.

"You made this in preschool!" Laura said. "I was so proud!"

A few ornaments were from trips abroad. Laura remembered their visit to Frankenmuth when Maya was little. They had gone for a ride in a horse-drawn carriage. Holding the ornament she had bought then brought on a wave of nostalgia. Maybe they could go to Michigan for Christmas next year.

"Are you excited about going to Max's house tomorrow?" Laura asked. She reminded herself that there were special times to be had in Japan.

"Yes," Maya said. "Max has promised to show me his dinosaur collection."

Laura had bought the candy cane cookies. Now, she took two from the box and put them on plates. She wanted to try one this time.

"Cookie time," she said. She poured two mugs of milk. She brought them to the coffee table in the living room, near the tree.

"Yay!" Maya said. "Thank you, Mommy!"

Laura bit into a cookie. She closed her eyes. It *did* taste a little different. What could that special ingredient be? Nutmeg? Anise? She really needed to figure it out, but she didn't have time before meeting up with Dr. Mori—Kazu—again.

11

The next afternoon, Laura dressed up in nice slacks. She put on a black sweater with a Santa motif. She wore short black leather boots instead of her usual Saturday sneakers. Maya was allowed to wear jeans and a sweatshirt. Who knew what the kids would be doing? They might be crawling around on the floor. Or running around outside.

When they were ready, Laura wrapped the box of cookies in a cloth. They set out for the nearest subway station. Using an app on her phone, Laura figured out which train they should take. They wormed their way through the underground crowds and managed to get a seat on the train.

A voice announced each stop in various languages. When they reached their stop, Laura and Maya got off. They found the exit and climbed the steps to street level. They walked the rest of the way, following the app's directions.

Kazu and Max lived in a house in a quiet neighborhood. When they found the address, Maya rang the bell. The door opened. Kazu appeared in a sweater appliqued with a moose. Laura grinned. They were both wearing holiday sweaters.

"Welcome," Kazu said, holding the door open.

Maya ran under his arm, off to join Max.

Laura paused. She suddenly felt a bit

shy. "These are for you," she said, handing over the cookies. She stepped inside.

She could smell coffee brewing.

"Great," Kazu said. He led her into the living room. "Have a seat. I will hang up your coats."

Laura took a look around. She had been curious, of course. The house was extremely neat. No LEGO blocks were on the floor. No newspapers or magazines were out of place. There were a few family photos in frames on a table.

Laura bent down to look at one of the photos. But first, she swiped her finger across the table. She brought it to her eyes. No dust! Then she turned her attention to the photo. A younger version of Kazu held a baby boy. He stood next to a frail-looking woman with blond hair and blue eyes.

Just then, Kazu entered the room. He was carrying a tray with cups of coffee on saucers. There was a little matching cream pitcher and a sugar bowl with tongs. The cookies were on a plate.

"Is that your wife?" Laura asked.

Kazu nodded. "Max barely remembers her, so I keep it out for him. I want to remind him that he had a mother who loved him."

Laura wondered if Kazu still missed his wife. Was he still mourning her?

"Your house is very tidy," she said.

"Thank you," Kazu looked down. A lock of hair fell across his forehead. Was that a blush? "I read one of your articles online. The one about housework and gender."

"Oh." He had done an online search on her? Should she be flattered or worried? She tried to remember if there were any embarrassing photos of her in cyberspace.

"I totally agree, by the way," he went on. "Japanese men should be equal partners. They should do more housework and childcare."

She had to admit, he was completely adorable.

"Well, you do it all!" she said. Actually, her own apartment was messy.

"Cookie?" he asked. He held out the plate.

"Thank you," she said.

He picked up a cookie and took a bite. "Mmmm. You really have to give me the recipe."

Laura hoped he would forget. Maybe once they got past Christmas he would stop bringing it up.

Just then, Max and Maya burst into the room. They both grabbed cookies from the plate and stuffed them into their mouths. Then Max said, "Hey Dad, do you know where Maria put my dinosaur costume after she washed it?"

Again, Kazu blushed. "Look in your pajama drawer," he told his son in a low voice. He avoided Laura's eyes.

Maria? Did Kazu have a girlfriend? Did she live here with them? Maria sounded Latina. What was the name of that woman who had been next to her at the bake sale? The one who had made the Mexican wedding cakes? Was this Maria another one of the international school mothers? Was Kazu a playboy?

Then again, he had never said that this was a date. They were here because of Maya and Max. This was just a play-date. It was a coffee klatch between parents.

Laura picked up another cookie and began to nibble. She was being silly. She had no right to be jealous. This was her chance to gather data about single Japanese men and housework.

She had all kinds of questions, but suddenly Max and Maya were back. This time they were dressed up as dinosaurs. They wanted to play Monopoly. Kazu cleared away the dishes so they could set up the board game.

There was no chance for Laura to ask questions.

– 13 –

On Monday, Laura sat at her desk. It was just before lunch. She stared at her computer screen. She thought about the playdate. Playing Monopoly had been fun, but she had wanted to talk to Kazu alone. Instead of putting hotels on Park Place, she wanted to ask him if he had had any relationships since his wife died. Did he think he might marry again? And who was Maria?

Laura had gone out on a few dates since her divorce. None had turned into relationships. One guy had taken her to dinner. Then he showed her a Pow-erPoint presentation of his trip to Bora-Bora. Was that the new dating style? She wasn't really interested in apps or dating sites. She could have hired a matchmaker. People did that in Japan. But she often felt that she was too busy for romance.

So why was she thinking about Kazu? Why was she wondering what it would be like to slip her hand into his? To snuggle up to him in front of a blazing fire? To rub her cheek against his?

"Knock knock!" Laura heard a man's voice. Someone was rapping on her door.

"Yes?" She tried to shake the fantasies from her head. She swiveled in her chair. Kazu stood in her doorway, as if summoned by her thoughts. He was wearing brown corduroys and a cream-colored sweater. That lock of hair fell over his forehead again. She wanted to comb it back with her fingers.

"Day off?" she said.

"I was in the neighborhood," he said. "I thought I would drop by."

"Come on in!" she said. She was suddenly aware of the piles of paper on her desk. A dirty coffee cup was in her sink. The wastebasket was full.

"Nice office. It's very c—"

"Cluttered? Chaotic?" Laura said with a laugh. "Yes, I know. But you should see my colleague's office. He has to enter sideways to get through the towers of books."

"Oh no," Kazu said. "I wasn't thinking that it was messy. More like cozy and comfortable."

"But you expected that someone who wrote about housework would be tidy," Laura said.

"Something like that," Kazu said. "But I am glad you are not obsessive." Then he showed her a plastic container. "I made some rugelach for you," he said. "And I was wondering if you would like to join me for lunch?"

"Thank you," Laura said. "And yes, I would love to!"

14

Laura and Kazu went to a nearby restaurant that sold thick udon noodles in broth. They sat at a low table in a booth on tatami mats. They left their shoes down below on the floor.

The server arrived to take their order.

"I will have the lunch set," Laura said in Japanese.

"Me too," Kazu added.

They switched to English. Likely no one would understand them. They could speak frankly.

"Where did you learn to speak English so well?" Laura asked.

"I studied dentistry in Oregon," Kazu said. "Americans have the best teeth. I figured I needed to study in the US."

Laura nodded.

"And what brought you to Japan?" Kazu asked.

Most Americans came to Japan these days because they were interested in manga and anime. Laura had studied Japanese court poetry. She had loved the idea of a culture where lovers had once communicated via poems. Even now, the emperor and empress wrote haiku and read them to the public each year.

"I was interested in Japanese literature," she said. "I came here to teach English. Then I fell in love. I got married. I had a child. Somewhere along the way, I became a professor."

"I met my wife in Portland," Kazu

said. "She was studying abroad, too. She did not speak Japanese. I could not speak Polish. We spoke in English. For me, English became the language of love."

His words made Laura sigh. Not only did he bake cookies, but he was also a romantic.

"Did you ever think of staying in the United States?" she asked him.

"Sometimes," he said. "But my family is here, and I wanted to be near them."

Laura wondered if Max ever got a chance to see his relatives in Poland.

"Yes, family is important," Laura agreed. She sometimes thought it would be better if she moved back to Michigan. She could see her parents and siblings at any time. But she wanted Maya to be able to see her father whenever she wanted.

Just then, the server brought a tray and set it before Kazu. She set another tray in front of Laura. Fragrant steam rose from the bowls of noodles. A ceramic dish cradled three pieces of tempura-fried vegetables. Another small dish held pickled radishes. And another, a square of chilled tofu topped with fish flakes.

"This looks delicious!" Laura said. She reached for a fused pair of disposable wooden chopsticks. According to Japanese superstition, if she broke them apart unevenly, she would not be able to marry. It was silly to think of this now. She had once been married. Now she was sitting across from an adorable single dad. She felt a tiny thrill when she managed to neatly separate the chopsticks.

"Are you going to the big Christmas pageant?" Kazu asked.

"Of course," Laura said.

Tokyo Cherry Blossom International School held an event showcasing the students' talents every year in mid-December. It was the last big hurrah before winter break.

"Do you want to sit together?" Kazu asked.

"Sure," Laura said. The year before, she had felt self-conscious sitting by herself. The Christmas pageant was held in the evening. It was the one event of the year that both mothers and fathers usually came to. She had invited Maya's dad, but his new wife had been pregnant. He had not shown up.

"I will save you a spot then," Kazu said. "That is, if I get there before you."

"And I will do the same," Laura promised. She wondered if the other moms would talk about them. Then again, maybe it would seem logical. The two single parents would be keeping each other company.

15

Laura shared the rugelach with Maya after school.

"Max's dad made this," Laura said. She paid careful attention to Maya's reaction. She was not sure how her daughter would feel if she dated her friend's dad.

Maya took a bite of the dried apricots, raisins, and walnuts rolled up in pastry. "Yummy!"

"We are going to sit together at the Christmas pageant," she went on. "Isn't that nice?"

Maya chewed and swallowed. "That reminds me!" She darted off to her room. She came back with red fabric, a piece of white fake fur, and some papers. "Here is the stuff that you need to make my costume. And the instructions."

Laura sighed. She wasn't particularly crafty, but she did have a sewing machine. At least this time Maya had not waited until the night before.

Over the next week, she taught her female students English by day. She spent the evenings stitching together Maya's costume. She had to tear everything apart and start over twice. Finally, she got on track. To keep up her holiday spirits, she streamed Christmas carols in the background.

She finished the costume just in time for the dress rehearsal. Some of the seams were puckered. The stitches were uneven. Oh well. No one would be able to tell from the audience. It was the best that Laura could do.

"Come over here. Try this on," Laura said.

It was late. Maya had already bathed. She was wearing her pink pajamas. Nevertheless, she twirled into the room. Laura settled the red fur-trimmed cape on her shoulders. She wrapped the matching skirt around Maya's hips. She had also made a hat with a pom-pom. Maya was instantly transformed into one of Santa's elves. So cute!

"Thanks, Mom. You're the best!" Maya said, giving her a kiss on the cheek.

16

Laura and Maya arrived at the school early on the evening of the Christmas pageant. "Break a leg!" Laura shouted.

Maya dashed off to her classroom to prepare.

Laura looked at the student artwork on the walls. The doily snowflakes glued to construction paper made her feel nostalgic. She liked the finger paintings with handprints converted into Hanukkah candles. She found Maya's signature in the corner of a painting of a reindeer. She took a photo of it with her phone.

Murmurs from the auditorium floated her way. The seats were filling up. She decided to go on in and claim spots for her and Kazu. When she walked into the spacious room, she saw that he had beaten her to it. He stood up from a seat near the front. He waved his hands to get her attention. Well, everyone would know they were sitting together now.

She waved back and made her way toward him.

"I got here a little bit early," he said. He cleared his coat from the empty chair next to his. "I wanted to make sure we got good seats."

Laura sat down beside Kazu. Every time she felt their elbows brush against each other, she was flooded with warmth.

Laura didn't know many of the other parents. Kazu seemed to have met everyone. Every few seconds, someone popped over to greet him. Every time he said, "And this is Dr. Murata, Maya's mom," the other parents raised their eyebrows and smirked. What did that mean? Was she one of the many single moms he had dated? And who was Maria?

She would not think about that. They were here to watch their kids. She looked at the stage. The curtains parted. The first grade students stood on risers. The children were all decked out in snowman costumes. They were ready to sing the first song.

Next, the fourth graders did a dance to the theme from the Disney movie *Frozen*. Then the second grade skit began. Maya was the star.

Kazu was recording the whole thing. Laura took photos. She was proud that Maya delivered her lines in a loud, clear voice. Max was great, too, hamming it up as an absentminded elf. The audience chuckled at all the right places. The parents clapped at the end. Laura was proud of Maya.

"Next stop Broadway, huh?" Kazu said, nudging Laura.

"They were so cute together, weren't they?" Laura said. And yes, she could imagine Maya becoming an actress. Why not?

"Did you make Max's costume?" she asked.

"Uhhh, I had a little help," Kazu confessed.

From that Maria person? It did not seem as if he wanted to explain. Laura decided to let it go. Thinking of Maria reminded Laura that she owed Kazu a playdate. He had invited her and her daughter over to his house. She should have Kazu and Max over to their apartment. It would give her a chance to redeem herself, too. She was still embarrassed about her messy office. If she knew that Kazu and Max were coming over, she would be able to tidy up in advance. She could even bake some cookies.

"What are you and Max doing this weekend?" Laura asked.

Kazu wrinkled his brow. "Max and I are going to see the new Godzilla movie on Sunday afternoon. We have no plans for Saturday."

"Do you want to come over? There is a park near our apartment. The kids could play. Then we could go back to my place for hot chocolate afterwards."

"That would be great," Kazu said.

They enjoyed the rest of the pageant. During the finale, the entire student body gathered on the stage to sing "We Are the World." After seven curtain calls, Laura and Kazu found their children.

"See you on Saturday!" Kazu said.

"Yes! I look forward to it!" Laura said.

17

Christmas was not an official holiday in Japan, so many universities held classes on Christmas Day. Luckily, Laura's classes ended the week before. She always took time off so that her winter vacation was at the same time as Maya's break. This year, she took a couple of extra days off. She wanted to get a jump start on her end-of-the-year cleaning and prepare for the weekend.

Laura had not yet figured out the secret ingredient in Emily's candy cane cookies. She decided to bake another kind. When she was a child, her mother always made different varieties. During the break, she and Maya would make cut-out cookies together. For now, she would whip up a batch of gingersnaps. It would be a nice surprise for Maya.

The apartment smelled like ginger and cloves. Maya came home from school.

"Don't forget to clean up your room," Laura told her. "Max and his dad are coming over tomorrow."

"Okay." Maya danced around the living room. She really did have a flair for the theatrical. "You really like him, don't you, Mom?"

"Who?" Laura blushed. Was it really that obvious? And had Maya and Max been gossiping about their parents at school? If so, the entire PTA probably knew about her feelings by now.

"You know," Maya said. "Dr. Mori! Max's dad!"

"Well, how would you feel about that?" Laura asked. Might as well not deny it, since she really did have a crush on him.

"Dr. Mori is nice, and he's good at baking," Maya said. "He's also very handsome. Go for it!"

Laura laughed. "I think we are just friends now. We will see what happens."

Now she had Maya's approval. But how did Kazu feel?

The sky was a clear blue on Saturday afternoon. Laura and Maya met up at a park near their apartment building with Kazu and Max. It was a leafy refuge in the middle of their Tokyo neighborhood. There was a swing set, slide, and jungle gym for the kids. There were brightly painted benches for the adults.

Laura and Kazu watched their kids climb and clamber, admiring their endless energy. They chatted about their own memories of tag and tree forts. Finally, the kids ran up to them.

"We're hungry," Maya and Max said.

"Let's go home and have a snack," Laura said.

As they walked back toward the apartment, she realized that they would be going past Emily's Sweet Shop. Maya did, too.

"Hey Mom," she shouted. She pointed to the American bakery. "Let's get some more of those candy cane cookies. Max really likes them."

Uh-oh. Busted. Laura couldn't bring herself to meet Kazu's eyes. Now he would know that she was a fraud.

18

"Ahh," Kazu said. "So that's why you could not give me the recipe."

"Yeah, I'm sorry I misled you," Laura said. "I have made candy cane cookies before. I really wanted to make them for the bake sale. But then I got busy at work. I forgot all about it. Maya reminded me the night before."

She snuck a look at his face. Okay, he did not look mad. He was studying the sidewalk, shoulders hunched forward. He looked as if he was getting ready to tell her a secret.

"Well, I guess I should come clean as well," he said. "The other day when you came over? And you said that our house looked so neat?"

"Yeah?" Laura responded.

"I did not clean it," Kazu said. "I asked Maria, Max's babysitter, to clean up for your visit." He looked up at Laura and gave her a sheepish smile. "I actually do not do a great job of keeping up with the housework."

Laura nodded.

"Sometimes I have to work late," Kazu went on. "Or there is some school holiday in the middle of the week when I have dental appointments. You know how it is. I don't like for Max to be home alone all the time."

"I understand completely," Laura said. "Maya usually hangs out in my office on school holidays, or tags along for conferences. I have also hired my students to babysit."

"Yeah, Max has spent his fair share of time at my dental practice," Kazu admitted.

"Did Maria bake the rugelach, too?" Laura asked. She was pretty sure she knew the answer.

"No, that was all me," Kazu said.

"It was delicious," Laura said. "I would love to have the recipe."

"You got it." He followed her to the apartment building. Laura keyed in a code to open the door. They all took the elevator upstairs.

When she opened the door, Max said, "Wow! A Christmas tree!"

"I have not gotten around to putting up a tree yet," Kazu said.

"And cookies!" Maya squealed.

Laura had already put some

gingersnaps out on a platter. She set the table with mugs and plates.

Kazu stepped into the living room area and took a look around. He scanned the titles on her bookshelf and checked out the photos. Laura was glad that she had dusted and vacuumed. She invited everyone to sit at the table. Kazu and Max took seats with a view of the tree.

"I do mean what I said," Kazu went on. "I really do believe that if couples live together, they should share chores. My wife and I tried to split up the work equally."

"Did you change diapers?" Laura asked.

"Absolutely," Kazu said. "And I potty trained Max all by myself."

"Dad!" Max frowned.

"Not while we're eating!" Maya said, helping herself to a gingersnap.

"I've been meaning to ask," Kazu said. "What are you doing Christmas Eve?"

"Oh, the usual. A bucket of fried chicken and Christmas cake." She and Maya opened presents on Christmas morning. Then they would make a Zoom call to her family in Michigan in the evening.

"I have an idea," Kazu said. His eyes twinkled.

"Yes?" Laura's stomach went flippity-flop. Was he going to suggest that they celebrate Christmas together? Like a family? She knew that New Year's was the time when families gathered in

Japan. Still, it would be special, wouldn't it?

"You can bring Maya over to my place on Christmas Eve. She and Max can enjoy fried chicken together," Kazu said.

"Oh right. That sounds great." Laura could not tell if she was being invited, too. Maybe it was a holiday playdate.

But there was more.

"I will get Maria, or somebody, to babysit," Kazu continued, "and you and I can have dinner at a fancy restaurant."

"Oh! Like a date?" Laura asked.

Max and Maya giggled. Kazu blushed.

"Yes," Kazu said. "A date."

Laura reminded herself that

Christmas Eve was the biggest date night of the year in Japan. It was bigger than Valentine's Day. This was a pretty big deal.

"I would love that," Laura said.

19

On Christmas Eve afternoon, Laura put on a sequined dress. Maya gathered the trading cards, manga, and video games that she would take over to Max's house. Usually, Laura made do with mascara and lip gloss. For this evening, she did up her eyes with black liner and eye shadow.

"Oh Mom," Maya said. "You look like a movie star!"

"Do you think so?" Laura laughed. "Well, thanks." She felt a shiver of anticipation. She hoped Kazu would react in the same way.

They took a taxi to Kazu and Max's house. As soon as the cab pulled up to the curb, Kazu stepped out the door. He was wearing a jacket with a black turtle-neck and gray trousers. He dashed out to pay the driver. He helped Laura out of the car.

"You look beautiful," he said.

"And you look pretty dapper your-self," she replied. He smelled nice, too.

Maya ran ahead and into the house. Her backpack bobbed on her back.

"Merry Christmas!" Max said. He was wearing a Santa hat. "Well, almost."

"Merry Christmas, Max!" Maya ran to the table. "Look, Mom! Christmas cake!"

A round cake covered with whipped cream and strawberries sat at the center of the table. It was already set with paper plates and cups. There was a bucket of fried chicken next to the cake.

Just then, a middle-aged woman with dark hair came into the room. "Hello," she said, wiping her hands on her apron.

"I'd like you to meet Maria," Kazu said to Laura. "She has been such a great help."

"Max is very sweet," Maria said. "He reminds me of my son when he was that age."

"I hope we're not keeping you from your family," Laura said.

"Not at all," Maria said. "My family is Jewish. We don't celebrate Christmas. You two have a nice time."

Kazu called for another taxi. "To Roppongi," he told the driver. They got into the car.

Night had already fallen. Blue and white lights twinkled in the trees along the streets. Christmas songs floated through the air. Off in the distance, they could see the orange Tokyo Tower, all lit up. Couples were everywhere. Their arms were linked. Their feet were in step. They were on their way to romantic dinners.

"Here is good," Kazu finally said.

The driver dropped them off in front of the Ritz-Carlton hotel. They took the elevator to the French restaurant on the forty-fifth floor. The hostess led them to a table by the window. The lights of Tokyo glittered below like a sea of diamonds.

"Oh, this is wonderful," Laura said. *And so romantic!*

Laura let herself wallow in luxury. One exquisite dish after another was set before her. She glanced at Kazu every now and then. They talked about everything except their kids and the international school. They found that they both loved nature documentaries, roller coasters, and llamas.

As he refilled her champagne glass, Kazu said, "You know, I think I may have figured out the secret ingredient in those candy cane cookies."

"Really? How?" Laura asked.

"Well, I had a hunch. I tried to bake a batch."

He had probably found a recipe online and tinkered with it. Well, good for him.

"What do you think it is?" Laura asked.

"Almonds," Kazu said.

"Hmmm. I think you might be right. In that case, I guess you no longer have any use for me," Laura teased. "Now you can make them on your own."

He reached across the table. He brushed his knuckles gently against her cheek. She wanted to lean into his hand like a kitten.

"Asking for the cookie recipe was just a ploy," Kazu said.

Laura laughed.

They finished their meal. Kazu said, "Shall we go down? Take a stroll? We can enjoy the illumination."

"Yes," Laura said. "That would be wonderful."

She thought that nothing could be more perfect than wandering arm in arm, admiring the lights. But then they stepped out onto the sidewalk. Kazu bent his head to hers for a kiss. And it began to snow.

CPSIA information can be obtained
at www.ICGtesting.com
Printed in the USA
JSHW082312180723
44953JS00002B/98